This book belongs to

....

D1403371

Copyright © 2014

make believe ideas ltd

The Wilderness, Berkhamsted, Hertfordshire, HP4 2AZ, UK.
501 Nelson Place, P.O. Box 141000, Nashville, TN 37214-1000, USA.

All rights reserved. No part of this publication may be reproduced,
stored in a retrieval system, or transmitted in any form or by any means,
electronic, mechanical, photocopying, recording, or otherwise, without
the prior written permission of the copyright owner.

www.makebelieveideas.com

Written by Fiona Boon.
Illustrated by Clare Fennell.
Designed by Sarah Vince.

The polar bear
who saved
Christmas

Fiona Boon · Clare Fennell

make
believe
ideas

One Christmas Eve, in a den in the snow,
a polar bear slept and so didn't know
that her cub was awake. Pip could not rest –

he was excited for Christmas,

the day he loved best!

In the **distance**, Pip heard a **jingling** sound.

He jumped up and **popped** his head above ground.

Pressed in the snow,

he saw **tracks** lead away.

He said to himself,

"It **must** be a **sleigh!**"

Pip walked through the snow
'til the jingling was gone.
Alone in the cold,
he soon missed his mom.
Fresh snow hid his paw prints
and covered the tracks.

With **no** path to follow,

would he **find** his way back?

But then the snow stopped,

and a blaze of bright light

led Pip to a strange and magical sight.

There were warm, cozy houses

and elves everywhere –

hope lifted the heart of the cold polar bear!

Pip peered through a window as he heard a loud wail:
"Dancer's broken her leg!
Who'll take Santa's mail?"
Inside was a sleigh filled with fine toys and treats.
Nearby, an elf shouted
and stamped
his small feet.

The reindeer were worried –
they felt at a loss!
The elf looked around
and said (getting cross),

"We have seven reindeer,
but our sleigh needs eight.
If we wait for Dancer,
it will be too late!"

As they pulled out the **sleigh**, the elves made a fuss –
what could they do to **save** this Christmas?

An elf soon saw Pip and said,

"Don't be shy!

Can you pull the sleigh?"

But Pip said,

"I can't fly!"

The elves said, "Don't worry!" and put Pip in line.

"With your help,
we'll certainly
make it in time."

They **sprinkled** some sparkles and Pip gave a **sneeze!**

He felt **brave** and knew it was now **time** to leave.

Santa jumped on
and took hold of the reins.
The reindeer leapt forward,
so Pip did the same.

The earth fell away as the huge sleigh took flight –

and Pip and the reindeer

flew off into the night.

They leapt across rooftops, delivering toys
to the homes of all the young girls and boys.

In bed, sound asleep,
no child was aware
that Santa's new helper
was a small polar bear!

Pip and the reindeer worked hard through the night, delivering joy on their magical flight.

The sleigh headed home when each gift was gone.
And though Pip was tired, they all cheered him on.

Then Pip saw his den – such a wonderful sight!
He slipped from the reins and took one final flight.

POLAR
BEAR
HOME

Cozy and warm

in the snow so deep,

curled up in his bed,

Pip fell straight asleep.

Early the next morning,

no tracks could be seen.

Pip looked around –

had it all been a dream?

But in the snow lay a note
and a shiny sleigh bell,

"For the bear who saved Christmas,
Santa wishes you well."